Dear Parent:

Congratulations! Your child is taking the first steps on an exciting journey. The destination? Independent reading!

STEP INTO READING® will help your child get there. The program offers five steps to reading success. Each step includes fun stories and colorful art. There are also Step into Reading Sticker Books, Step into Reading Math Readers, Step into Reading Phonics Readers, Step into Reading Write-In Readers, and Step into Reading Phonics Boxed Sets—a complete literacy program with something for every child.

Learning to Read, Step by Step!

Ready to Read   Preschool–Kindergarten
• big type and easy words • rhyme and rhythm • picture clues
For children who know the alphabet and are eager to begin reading.

Reading with Help   Preschool–Grade 1
• basic vocabulary • short sentences • simple stories
For children who recognize familiar words and sound out new words with help.

Reading on Your Own   Grades 1–3
• engaging characters • easy-to-follow plots • popular topics
For children who are ready to read on their own.

Reading Paragraphs   Grades 2–3
• challenging vocabulary • short paragraphs • exciting stories
For newly independent readers who read simple sentences with confidence.

Ready for Chapters   Grades 2–4
• chapters • longer paragraphs • full-color art
For children who want to take the plunge into chapter books but still like colorful pictures.

STEP INTO READING® is designed to give every child a successful reading experience. The grade levels are only guides. Children can progress through the steps at their own speed, developing confidence in their reading, no matter what their grade.

Remember, a lifetime love of reading starts with a single step!

Visit us on the Web!
StepIntoReading.com
rhcbooks.com

Educators and librarians, for a variety of teaching tools, visit us at RHTeachersLibrarians.com

ISBN 978-0-525-64797-3

Printed in the United States of America

10 9 8 7 6 5 4 3

STEP INTO READING®

nickelodeon

SEVEN RUFF-RUFF RESCUES!

PAW PATROL™

A Collection of Seven
Step 1 and Step 2 Early Readers

Random House 🏠 New York

CONTENTS

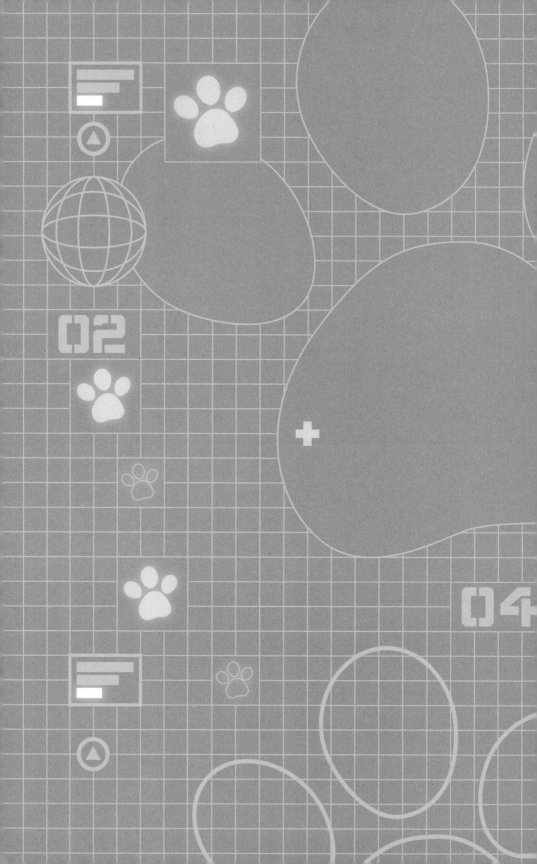

PAW PATROL™

MISSION PAW

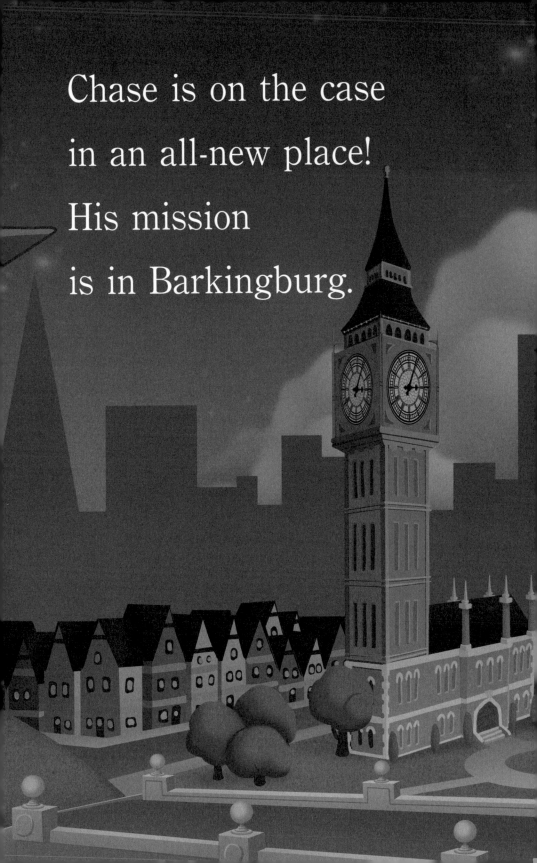

Chase is on the case
in an all-new place!
His mission
is in Barkingburg.

In Barkingburg,
Chase meets the princess
and the earl.

He also meets
the royal dog.
Her name is Sweetie.

Chase guards

the Barkingburg crown.

Sweetie puts on the crown. She wants to be queen!

Chase sees Sweetie
wearing the crown.
His bow tie is
a camera.
He makes a video.

Sweetie stops Chase!
He is locked
in the dungeon!
He calls
for help.

PAW Patrol
to the rescue!

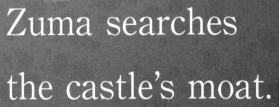

Zuma searches
the castle's moat.

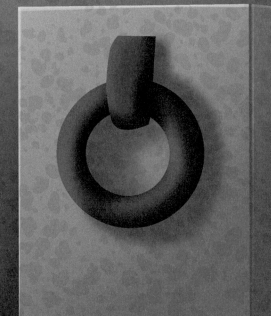

Knock, knock, knock!

Zuma hears something.

Is Chase knocking on

the wall?

Rubble's Mini Miner can help!

Rubble drills through
the castle wall.

Chase is safe!

Chase shows his video
to the earl and the princess.
They learn that Sweetie
took the crown.

Sweetie tries to escape.

Skye stops her.

The crown is safe again!

Chase, Skye,
Marshall, Rubble,
and Zuma
are all good pups!

28

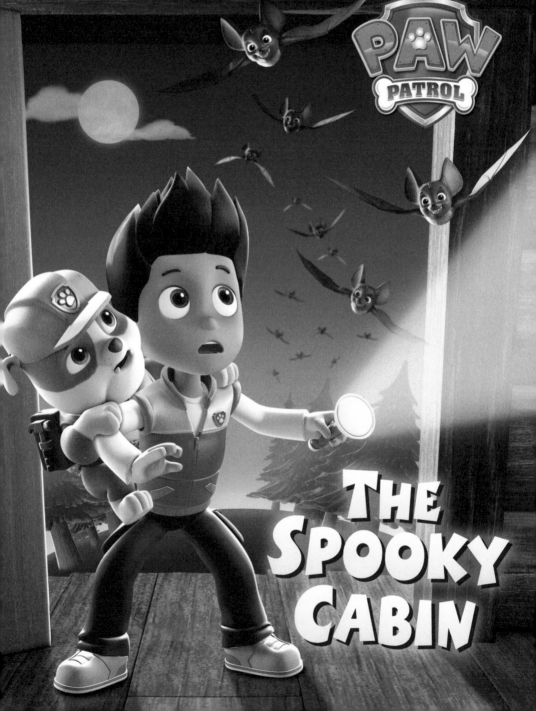

STEP INTO READ

nick

PAW PATROL

THE SPOOKY CABIN

30

Jake is fixing up
an old cabin.
Rocky and Rubble
are helping him.

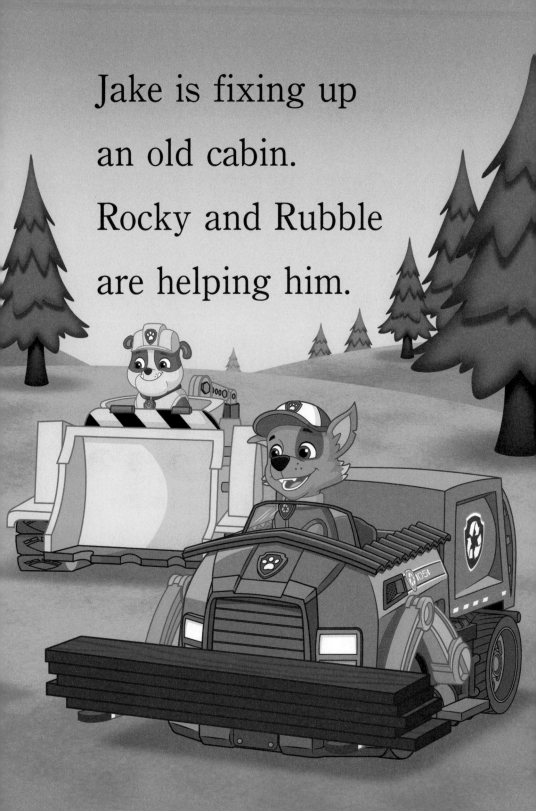

It is lunchtime.

Uh-oh!

Rubble's food

is gone!

Jake's lunch box floats
into the cabin.

Is a ghost moving it?

Jake calls Ryder

for help.

Ryder and Chase
race to the cabin.

Boom!

The porch
falls down!

Rocky finds some posts
to fix the porch.
Don't lose it—reuse it!

The pups fix
the porch!

Everyone goes
inside the cabin.
It is dark and spooky.
Bats fly through
the air.

Rubble falls into

a secret door.

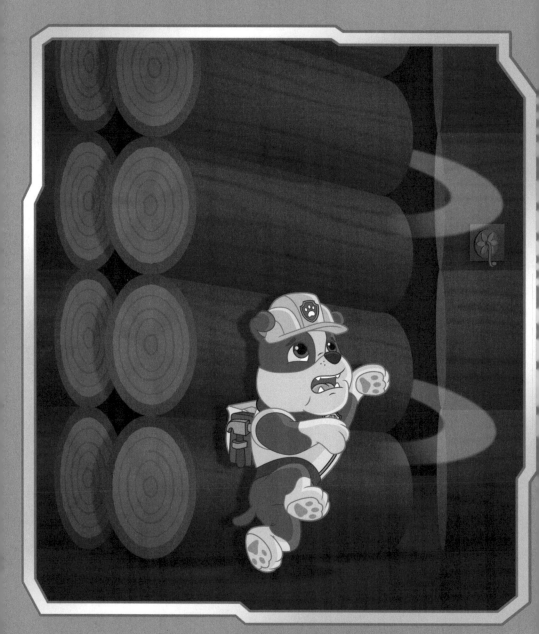

Rubble is missing.
Rocky thinks a ghost
grabbed him.
Ryder does not believe
in ghosts.

Outside, Chase's spy drone
flies over the cabin.

Chase sees that Rubble
is still inside the cabin.
Rubble is not alone!

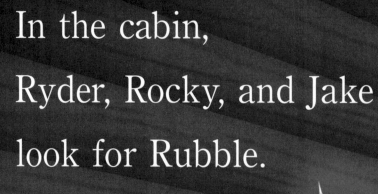

In the cabin,
Ryder, Rocky, and Jake
look for Rubble.

Lights go on and off.

Paintings move.

Ryder pushes a button.

It opens

the secret door.

Rubble is free!

Rocky sees mice
on the floor.
Ryder solves
the mystery!

The cabin is not haunted.
The mice make the lights
go on and off.

The mice make the paintings move. They also tickle Rubble's paws!

The pups build
a little cabin for the mice.
Whenever you
are in trouble,
just squeak for help!

PAW PATROL

Meet Tracker!

Carlos is in the jungle.
He is digging
for lost treasure.

The PAW Patrol
will visit Carlos.

Carlos trips.

He drops his phone!

Carlos is in
a deep pit.
He yells for help.

A pup hears Carlos.

He runs to help.

His name is Tracker.

Tracker finds

Carlos's phone.

He calls the PAW Patrol.

They will help Carlos.

A snake!

Tracker is not afraid.
He chases the
snake away!

PAW Patrol to the rescue!

Chase pulls Carlos
out of the pit.
Carlos is safe!

Because he helped Carlos,
Tracker gets to join
the PAW Patrol!

Tracker gets a Pup Pack.

It has cool tools!

Ropes spring from

Tracker's pack.

Tracker swings through the trees on his ropes!

Tracker gets
his own truck, too!

Welcome to the team, Tracker!

STEP INTO REAI

nic

PAW
PATROL

RUBBLE'S BIG WISH

Rubble and Rocky
find an old box.
Rubble wants
to clean it up.
He takes a nap first.

Rubble has a dream.
He turns the handle
on the box.
A genie named Jeremy
pops out!
The box is magic!

The genie will give
Rubble three wishes.

Rubble wishes

for a bone

that will last forever.

The genie uses his magic.
A giant bone appears
in the sky!

Oh, no!
The bone crashes
through the roof
of the barn.

Rubble will
fix the roof.
The PAW Patrol
will help!

Rubble lifts the bone
with his crane.

Skye flies Rocky
to the roof.

Rocky fixes the roof.

Jeremy the genie helps.

The roof is fixed!

The pups chew

on the giant bone.

Oops!
Rubble falls
into a mud puddle.
He is so dirty!

Jeremy says Rubble
has two wishes left.
Rubble wishes
for a super bubble bath!

Rubble loves
his bubble bath.
It is so bubbly,
it floats away!

Oh, no! Rubble's tub gets stuck in a tree.

The PAW Patrol will help!

Skye lowers Ryder.

He grabs Rubble

just in time.

Rubble has
one wish left.
He uses it
to thank his friends.

Jeremy flies
into the sky.
He gives the pups
tons of treats!

Rubble is happy
to share his wish
with his friends.

Rubble wakes up.

What a yummy dream!

nickelodeon

PAW PATROL

EVEREST SAVES THE DAY!

The pups are going
on a trip.

They will ride in
the PAW Patroller.

Robo Dog will drive
the PAW Patroller.
All the pups
are excited.

Just then, Jake calls.

He can't wait

to see the pups.

They are going to visit
him at the Ice Fields.

Suddenly, Jake slips
on the ice.

His pack slides

into a river!

Jake is in trouble!
The pups roll
their trucks onto
the PAW Patroller.

It is time to race

to the Ice Fields.

Meanwhile, Jake
slides toward
the river.
A pup saves him!

The pup's name
is Everest.
She is a husky
and a hero!

Chase and Ryder
search the Ice Fields.
They find Jake's tracks.

At the same time,

Skye searches

from the air.

She sees something!

Jake and Everest

cross an ice bridge.

Crack! Crack!

Oh, no!
The ice bridge
is breaking!

Jake falls!

Everest grabs him!

Jake is safe.

Everest gets a badge.
Now she is part
of the PAW Patrol!

Hooray for Everest!

She is one cool pup!

nickelodeon

PAW PATROL

Up in the AIR!

Ryder and the pups
are camping in the forest.
They hear a sound
in the sky.

Ace the pilot,
Mayor Goodway,
and Chickaletta
soar by in a plane!

Ace is teaching

the mayor how to fly.

The mayor swerves
around a flock of birds.
A wing on the plane breaks!

Ace must fix
the wing!
The mayor steers
the plane.

Ace's sleeve gets caught
on the broken wing!

Ace and the mayor
need help!
They call
the PAW Patrol.

Ryder takes the call.

He tells the pups to get

to the Air Patroller!

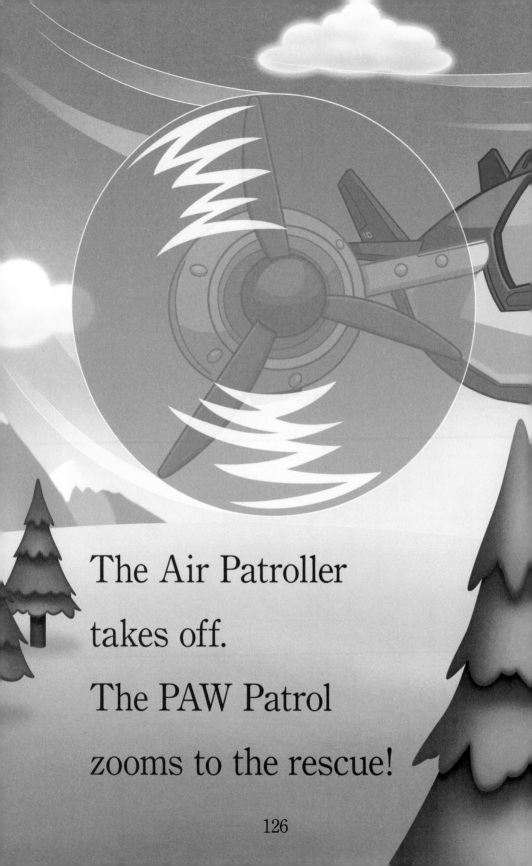

The Air Patroller
takes off.
The PAW Patrol
zooms to the rescue!

Meanwhile, Ace's plane shakes in the wind. Chickaletta bounces out onto the wing!

The Air Patroller
hovers over Ace's plane.
Skye and Rocky
fly down.

Skye flies Ace's plane.

She is a great pilot.

Rocky uses scissors.

Snip! Snip!

He cuts Ace's sleeve.

He frees Ace!

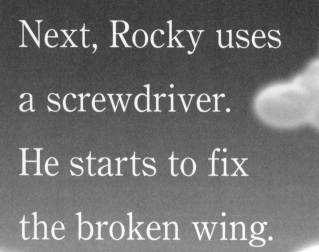

Next, Rocky uses
a screwdriver.
He starts to fix
the broken wing.

Ace tries to save Chickaletta.
She reaches for Chickaletta,
but the chicken falls
off the wing!

Marshall dives
from the Air Patroller.
He soars through
a flock of birds.

Marshall catches

Chickaletta on his head!

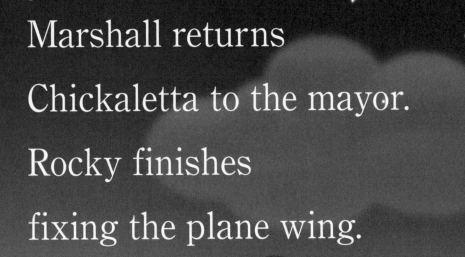

Marshall returns
Chickaletta to the mayor.
Rocky finishes
fixing the plane wing.

The PAW Patrol saved
Ace, the mayor,
and Chickaletta!
They all roast
marshmallows
to celebrate.

PAW
PATROL®

Under the
Waves!

The PAW Patrol is
also the Sea Patrol!
They are ready
to protect the beach.

Rocky does not like
to get wet.
He will not swim!

Cap'n Turbot is out
on his boat.
He does not see a
baby octopus stuck
to his bucket.

Suddenly,
an octopus appears!
It grabs the boat.

Cap'n Turbot needs help.

He calls Ryder.

The Sea Patrol is on a roll!
The pups hop aboard a ship.
Ryder tells Robo Dog
where to go.

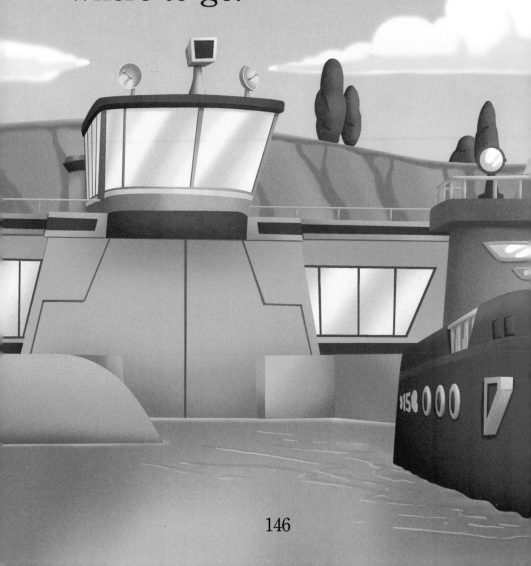

Robo Dog steers
the PAW Patroller
to Cap'n Turbot's boat.

Zuma tries
to free the boat.
The big octopus
is too strong!

Ryder blows the
PAW Patroller's horn.
The octopus is surprised.
It lets go of
the boat.

But the boat begins to sink!

Rubble uses his crane.
He lifts Cap'n Turbot
out of the water.
The baby octopus
is stuck to
the captain's life ring.

Marshall puts on scuba gear.

He dives into the water.

He pumps air into the boat.

The boat lifts!

Marshall swims
under the waves.
He finds
a baby rattle.

Back on the beach,
the baby octopus
jumps onto the
mayor's head!

The octopus
rises out of the water.
She is looking
for her baby!

The Sea Patrol
needs to get
the baby octopus
back to its mama fast!

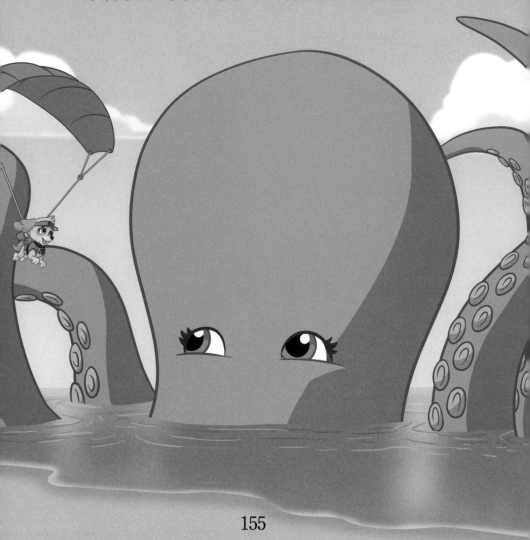

Marshall waves the rattle.
The baby octopus
reaches for it.
But the mayor knocks the
rattle into the sea!

Rocky wants to help.

He dives into the sea.

He is getting wet!

He finds the rattle

with his metal detector.

Ryder and
Zuma shake the rattle.
They lead the baby
octopus to its mother!

The family is
together again!

Hooray for the Sea Patrol!
And hooray for Rocky!
Now he likes
to get wet.